FAIRIES OF THE FOREST

STORY BY

LINDA BLACKMOOR

ISBN: 979-8-9884084-8-2 (PRINT)

PUBLISHED BY QUILL PRESS. LINDA BLACKMOOR'S TITLES MAY BE
PURCHASED IN BULK FOR EDUCATIONAL, BUSINESS, FUNDRAISING, OR
SALES PROMOTIONAL USE. FOR INFORMATION, PLEASE EMAIL
HELLO@LINDABLACKMOOR.COM

FIRST PRINT EDITION: 2024

LINDA BLACKMOOR
WWW.LINDABLACKMOOR.COM

IN THE ENCHANTED WOODLANDS,
WHERE SUNLIGHT DANCES UPON LEAVES,
IF YOU LOOK EVER SO CLOSELY THROUGH THE BRANCHES,
YOU MAY SPOT FLUTTERS OF DRESSES AND WINGS,
HEAR SOFT GIGGLES MUFFLED BY THE WIND IN THE CANOPY,
AND CATCH **THE FOREST FAIRIES** AMONGST THE TREES.

THE FOREST FLOOR IS DOTTED WITH MUSHROOMS,
TURKEY TAILS REST ON MOSS-COVERED LOGS,
WHILE TASTY MORELS NESTLE AMONG WILDFLOWERS,
AND AMANITAS SHADE SMALL TOADS AND MICE.
HERE, **THE MUSHROOM FAIRIES** CARE FOR EACH CAP,
BLESSING THEM WITH HEALING MAGIC.

FROM THE SPOTTED FAWN AT REST IN A BED OF GRASS,
TO THE CUNNING RED-FOX DARTING BETWEEN THE TREES,
THE WILDLIFE FAIRIES CARE FOR THEIR BEASTLY FRIENDS.
UNDER THEIR WATCHFUL EYES, THE FAUNA THRIVE.
THEY HELP TEACH THE ANIMALS HOW TO HUNT AND FORAGE,
GUIDING THEM TO CREEKS FOR A REFRESHING DRINK.

FROM THE BUMBLING, BUZZING BEES,

TO THE GRACEFUL BUTTERFLIES AND MYSTICAL LUNA MOTHS,

TO THE FIREFLIES THAT ILLUMINATE THE FOREST AT NIGHT,

THE BUG FAIRIES TEND TO THE SMALLEST BEINGS,

CRUCIAL FOR THE ECOSYSTEM'S VITALITY.

THEY KEEP THE WOODLAND REALM VIBRANT AND ALIVE.

THE TOWERING OAKS AND THE EVERGREEN PINES,
AND THE ANCIENT MAPLES, RICH WITH SWEET SAP,
TO THE WILLOWS THAT SWAY WITH A DANCER'S GRACE,
THE TREE FAIRIES WEAVE THEIR MAGIC IN FOREST CATHEDRALS.
NURTURING EVERY SAPLING AND ANCIENT BARK,
THEY KEEP THE CANOPIES LUSH AND THE ROOTS STRONG.

FROM THE BABBLING BROOKS TO THE GENTLE RAIN,
AND THE SMALL PONDS MIRRORING THE SKY'S ENDLESS BLUE,
TO THE DEWDROPS SPARKLING ON LEAVES AND PETALS,
THE WATER FAIRIES DANCE IN RAINBOWS REFLECTED IN STREAMS,
GUIDING EACH CREEK AND BLESSING EVERY RAINDROP,
THEY HELP NOURISH ALL LIFE IN THE WOODLANDS.

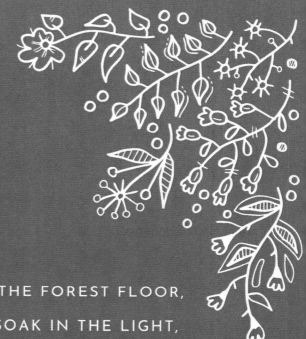

THE VELVETY MOSS THAT CARPETS THE FOREST FLOOR,

AND THE FERNS THAT UNFURL TO SOAK IN THE LIGHT,

TO THE LICHENS THAT CLING TO ROCKS AND BARK,

THE PLANT FAIRIES NURTURE THE FLORA OF THE UNDERBRUSH.

THEY BALANCE THE MOISTURE, ENRICH THE SOIL,

PROMOTING GROWTH AND LUSH VIBRANT LEAVES.

SOMETIMES YOU'LL SEE THEM IN A GENTLE BREEZE,
OR IN THE POWERFUL GUSTS BENDING TREES,
THE WIND FAIRIES ARE VITAL TO THE FOREST'S BREATH,
CARRYING SEEDS AND POLLEN ALONG THEIR WINDING PATH.
THEY AID PLANTS IN BREATHING OXYGEN AND CARBON DIOXIDE,
AND BALANCING A PLEASANT TEMPERATURE.

SPRING BURSTS IN VIBRANT COLORS ACROSS THE FOREST.
THE FLOWER FAIRIES GENTLY TEND THE FRAGILE BLOOMS.
TALL FOXGLOVES FEED THE BUSY HONEYBEES,
AND WILD ROSES UNFURL THEIR PINK AND RED PETALS,
WHILE THE ELDERFLOWERS SWEETLY PERFUME THE AIR.
FAIRIES CRAFT THEIR FAVORITE FLOWERS INTO DRESSES.

THE SUN'S WARMTH FEELS LIKE HONEY IN THE FOREST,
DANCING THROUGH BRANCHES TO REACH THE SOIL.
ANIMALS AND PLANTS BASK IN ITS EMBER GLOW.
THE SUN FAIRIES WEAVE THE LIGHT THROUGH THE TREES,
HELPING THE PLANTS GROW TALL AND HEALTHY,
AND WELCOMING THE DAY SO THAT LIFE CAN BLOOM.

NIGHTFALL BLANKETS THE FOREST IN DARKNESS.
THE NIGHT FAIRIES AWAKEN THE NOCTURNAL ANIMALS,
REMINDING THEM IT'S TIME TO START THEIR HUNT FOR FOOD.
AS NIGHT SETTLES THE DAY INTO SILENCE,
IN THE GLOW OF THE STARS AND THE MOON,
THE FOREST STILL TEEMS WITH LIFE.

THOUGH SOME FOREST FAUNA MAY PREFER GRUB,

MANY LOVE THE SWEET TASTE OF BERRIES.

THE FRUIT FAIRIES ARE TASKED TO HELP THESE BERRIES GROW.

FROM THE ELDERBERRY TO THE RASPBERRY TO THE BLUEBERRY,

EVEN THE TREES BEAR WILD APPLES TO EAT,

THIS GIVES THE WOODLAND CRITTERS A TASTY TREAT.

THE **<u>SEASON FAIRIES</u>** USHER CHANGE INTO THE FOREST,

SPRING ADORNS THE FOREST WITH VIBRANT BLOOMS,

SUMMER BLESSES IT WITH WARMTH FOR DELICIOUS FRUITS TO GROW,

AUTUMN SETS THE WOODLANDS ABLAZE IN FIERY HUES,

AND WINTER CLOAKS THE FOREST IN FROST, ENCOURAGING REST,

THE FAIRIES OF THE FOREST WORK TOGETHER IN HARMONY.

Made in the USA
Las Vegas, NV
01 June 2024

90618301R00021